EGMONT

We bring stories to life

First published in Great Britain 2012 by Dean,
an imprint of Egmont UK Limited
239 Kensington High Street, London W8 6SA

HiT entertainment

© 2012 Prism Art & Design Limited,
a HIT Entertainment company.
Based on an original idea by D. Gingell,
D. Jones and original characters created by R. J. M. Lee.

ISBN 978 0 6035 6759 9
53026/1
Printed in Italy

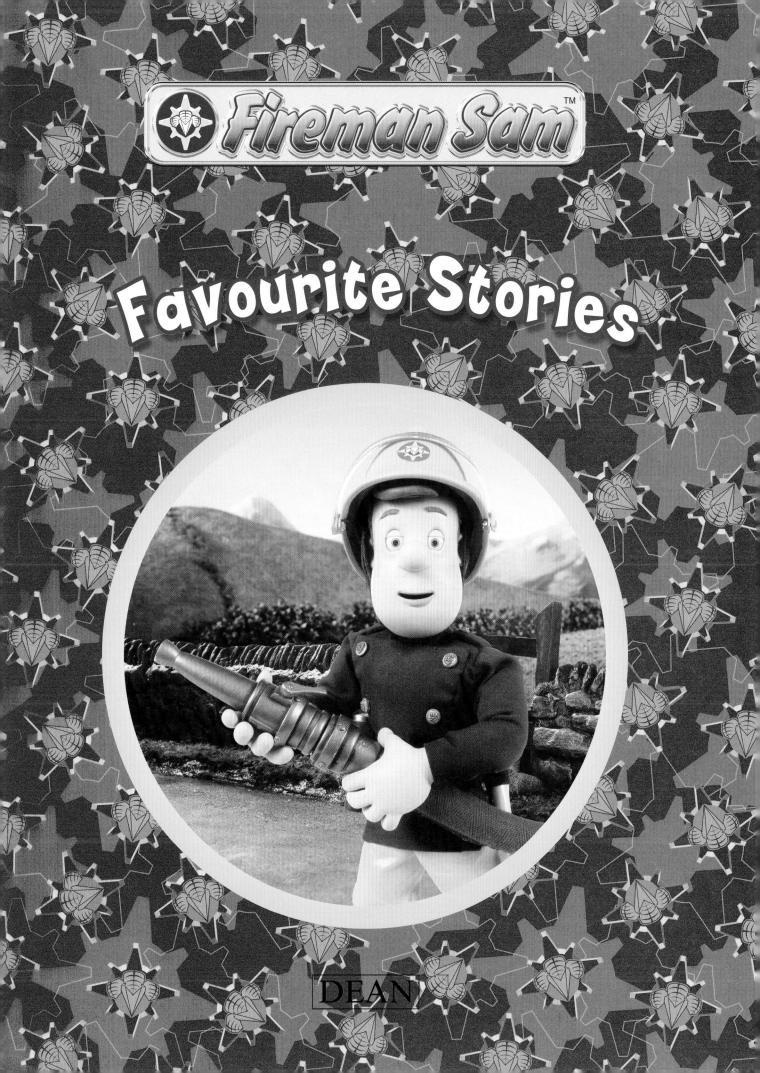

Fireman Sam™

Favourite Stories

DEAN

This book
belongs to

....

Contents

Fields of Fire

Fireman Sam was blowing up an inflatable dam outside the Fire Station. "What have you got there, Sam?" asked Trevor.

"It's an inflatable dam," said Sam. "It is used to store water when we're fighting a fire and there's no tap nearby."

"I'd love to see it in action," replied Trevor. "But I'm taking Mandy and Norman to the seaside." He jumped into his bus, and waved goodbye.

As Trevor drove through the countryside, the bus exhaust made a loud bang. "Did you just sit on a balloon, Mr Evans?" giggled Norman.

"Very funny, Norman," replied Trevor. "But it won't be so funny if the bus breaks down!"

Suddenly the bus made three loud bangs, and little puffs of smoke came out of the exhaust, before it stopped.

Trevor got off the bus and looked underneath the bonnet. "I'm going to try to fix it," Trevor said to the children. "Wait there – don't wander off!"

Meanwhile, Norman and Mandy noticed a funny sign near the gate.

After working out that it meant 'no campfires', they realised Dusty was missing! Hearing a bark in the distance, the children ran to find him.

In the countryside, Dusty was barking loudly as he chased a fieldmouse. Norman and Mandy spotted him and were close behind.

"Look! Someone hasn't put their campfire out," said Mandy, as she spotted a smoking fire on the ground. "We should tell Trevor."

"Let's find Dusty first," said Norman. The two children chased off after Dusty, just as the campfire set alight again!

Norman and Mandy chased after Dusty and finally caught up with him. They stopped suddenly and landed in a heap on the floor.

"It's gone really foggy," said Norman, as smoke billowed across them.

"That's not fog, Norman, it's smoke!" Mandy realised.
"It must be that campfire!"

"Mr Evans! Help!" Norman and Mandy shouted.

On the roadside, Trevor had fixed the bus. He could faintly hear Norman and Mandy calling out in the distance.

Trevor looked over the wall and saw smoke rising from the field.

"Oh my goodness!" he cried. Trevor quickly dialled 999 on his phone.

At the Fire Station, Station Officer Steele picked up the emergency message. "Action Stations, everyone!" he said. "A field is burning on the coast road, and Norman and Mandy are stuck in it!"

"There's no water for miles around there!" said Fireman Sam. "Elvis, you load the dam and I'll radio Tom at Mountain Rescue."

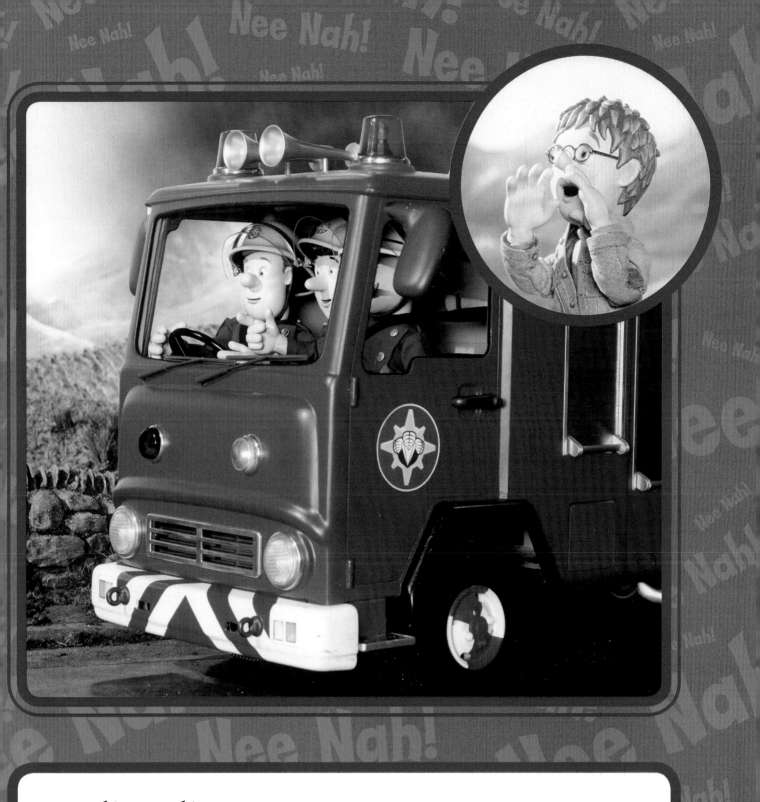

Nee Nah! Nee Nah! The fire engine Jupiter raced along the country lanes with its lights flashing. It stopped next to Trevor and his bus.

Sam, Elvis and Station Officer Steele leapt out and headed across the field with the hoses and the dam. The field was filled with thick smoke.

"Help! Help! We're over here!" shouted Norman.

Meanwhile, Tom Thomas was flying over Pontypandy Lake in his helicopter, Wallaby One. The helicopter was carrying a huge bucket. It swooped down, lowering the bucket carefully into the lake.

"I'm picking up the water now! Be with you in two minutes, Sam!" said Tom into his headset. Then he set off towards the field.

Meanwhile, the officers had set up the dam.

"Right, men. I'll supervise the water drop," said Officer Steele.

Tom lowered the bucket towards the inflatable dam.

"Left a bit, Tom. That's it!" said Officer Steele, tipping the water into the dam. "Now, Sam, Elvis, find those children!"

Carrying hoses and breathing apparatus, they walked into the smoke.

Sam and Elvis set their hoses on the fire and soon the smoke started to billow away. Dusty raced towards them and Norman and Mandy trooped sadly alongside.

"Thank goodness you're alright!" said Sam. "You gave us quite a fright wandering off like that."

"Sorry, Sam," said Norman and Mandy.

It was too late to go to the seaside, but Sam told everyone to go to the Fire Station instead. When they arrived, it looked just like a beach!

Tom's helicopter flew overhead to top up the dam. Elvis quickly grabbed the bucket, tipping water all over Station Officer Steele!

"Hee, hee!" giggled Norman and Mandy.

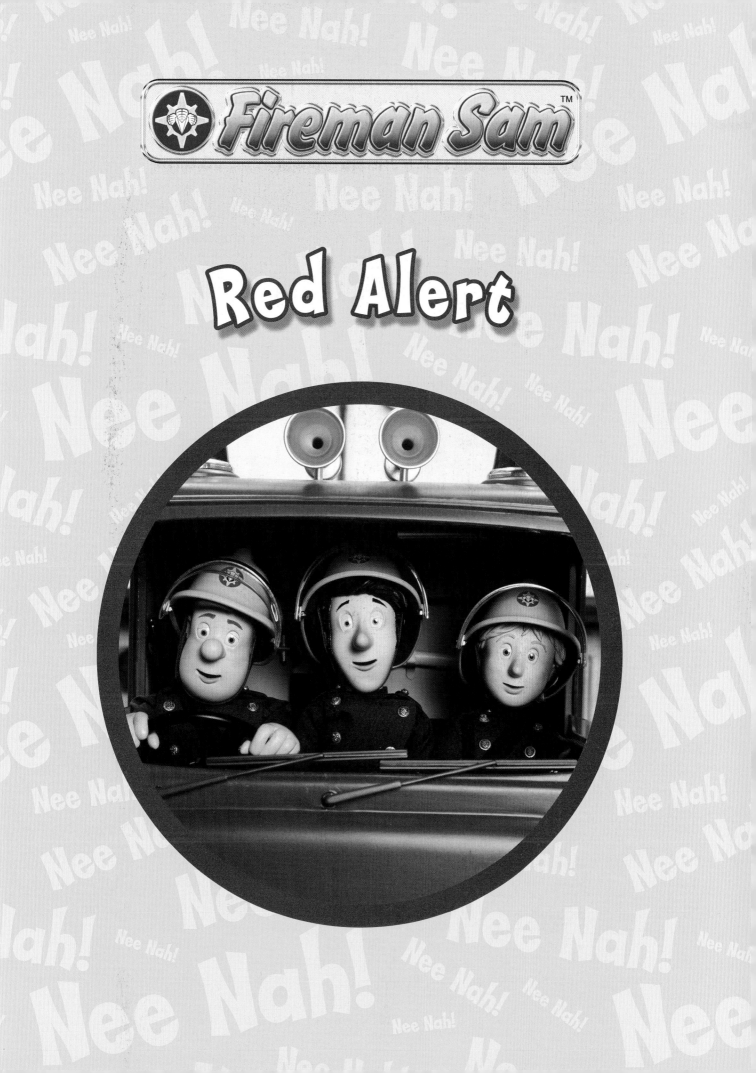

Fireman Sam™

Red Alert

One hot summer's day, Station Officer Steele was talking to his crew.

"This warm summer has left us with a big problem," Station Officer Steele began. "The grass around Pontypandy is as dry as a desert, making it very easy for a fire to start."

"We'll be on red alert, Sir," said Fireman Sam.

Norman Price and Mandy Flood were out walking near Pontypandy Mountain. They were looking for Woolly, Norman's pet sheep.

"Cor, it ain't half hot," said Norman, mopping his brow.

"Let's stop for a rest," said Mandy. "Tracking Woolly is thirsty work!"

Norman took a bottle of fizzy pop and began to gulp it down.

"**BURP!**" he went, when he'd finished drinking.

"Norman!" giggled Mandy.

"Sorry!" said Norman. "Did you want a drink, too?"

"No, thanks!" smiled Mandy. "Come on, let's go and find Woolly."

"I think I heard Woolly bleating over this way," said Mandy. "Come on!"

Norman ran to catch her up. He didn't notice when the empty pop bottle fell out of his rucksack and landed near a patch of dry grass.

The hot sun began to shine on the glass bottle and before long, a spark appeared, setting the grass on fire!

Meanwhile, Dilys Price and Trevor Evans had gone bird-watching. As they sat in the hut, Trevor was using his binoculars to look for birds. Suddenly, he spotted Woolly the sheep!

"I've seen lots of different types of birds here," said Trevor. "But I didn't know we were sheep-watching, too!"

"BAAA!" went Woolly, as he wandered past.

Soon after, Norman and Mandy appeared by the hut.

"Hi, Mam!" Norman shouted. "We didn't know you were here!"

"Shh! You're frightening the birds away!" said Trevor.

"Sorry, Trevor," called Norman. "Sorry, Mam!"

"Come on, Norman. Woolly must be somewhere around here," said Mandy, waving goodbye to Dilys and Trevor.

Norman and Mandy looked everywhere, but Woolly was nowhere to be seen. They stopped for lunch when suddenly, Woolly appeared!

"See. Never could resist a jammy dodger!" laughed Norman.

Mandy sniffed the air. "Hey, Norman! Can you smell smoke?"

Norman's glass bottle had started a fire which was spreading towards the hut! Trevor and Dilys ran clear, just as it collapsed behind them.

Norman quickly ran to the phone box to call for help.

At Pontypandy Fire Station, Fireman Sam picked up the emergency message. "Action Stations! There's a fire by the bird-watching hut," he said.

In seconds flat, Jupiter was heading out of the Fire Station with Sam, Elvis and Penny in the cab.

They had almost reached the fire when suddenly, there was a loud "**BANG!**" and Jupiter screeched to a halt.

A sharp rock in the road had punctured one of Jupiter's tyres!

"Elvis, Penny, you change the wheel," Sam said.
"I'll radio for Tom to come with his helicopter."

Norman and Mandy were feeling very afraid, when suddenly they heard Tom's helicopter overhead! "Over here!" they waved.

When Tom's helicopter was in position above the fire, he opened a chute, releasing special red water. It put out the fire at once.

Poor Norman was standing too close and got soaked by the red water! "Aargh! Tom!" he moaned, as Mandy giggled from behind a tree.

Moments later, Fireman Sam and the crew arrived. They checked that the fire was out, then cleared away the burnt wood and glass bottle.

"All safe and sound again!" said Sam.

"Oh dear," said Trevor, looking at the ruined hut. "I don't think we'll be doing any more bird-watching for a while!"

"Norman, it was your pop bottle that caused the fire," explained Sam. "I hope that you've learnt your lesson."

"Sorry, Sam," said Norman. "I'll be really careful not to leave glass bottles lying around in the sun again." He was covered from head to toe in the red liquid and feeling very sorry for himself.

"It's lucky we were on red alert!" Fireman Sam chuckled.

Deep Trouble

In the Fire Station garden, Norman and Mandy had come to visit Fireman Sam in his special inventing shed.

"Cor, what's that you've made, Sam?" asked Norman.

"This is my new super-duper beep-o-matic metal detector," said Sam. "If there's treasure to be found, this will find it!"

Beep! Beep! Beep! went the beep-o-matic.

When Sam had gone indoors, Norman ran over to the metal detector.

"Come on, Mandy!" Norman cried. "Let's go treasure-hunting in Pontypandy Mountain!"

"Shouldn't we ask Sam first?" worried Mandy.

"Oh, he won't mind," said Norman, cheekily. He took a coin out of his pocket and held it up. "We might even find some ancient coins!"

Up on Pontypandy Mountain, Norman and Mandy started their treasure hunt in the middle of an old stone circle.

"Let's try here," said Norman, swinging the beep-o-matic into action.

"Norman, did you feel that?" gasped Mandy. "The ground just went all wobbly!"

Beep! Beep! Beep! went the beep-o-matic metal detector.

"Don't worry, that must mean there's treasure down below. Let's get digging!" ordered Norman. He took out his trowel and began to dig.

"Ugh, I just got a mouthful of dirt!" said Mandy. "Let me have a go!"

"Sorry, Mandy!" said Norman, turning around to hand her the trowel.

Suddenly, the ground gave way . . . a large hole appeared . . . and poor Mandy disappeared down it!

"Help!" cried Mandy, from the bottom of the hole.

Norman shone his torch down into the deep, dark hole. He could see Mandy sitting at the bottom.

"Mandy?" said Norman, spinning round. "Are you all right?"

"I think so," she whimpered. "It's so cold and dark, I can't see a thing."

"Hang on, Mandy," shouted Norman. "I've got an idea!"

He went to his rucksack and took out a long rope. He tied one end of the rope around the torch and lowered it to the bottom of the hole.

"Got it!" called Mandy. "Thanks, Norman!"

Mandy shone the torch around the cave and to her surprise, there was a glittering display of treasure!

"Wow!" Mandy shouted. "You'll never guess what I've found!"

But Norman had already run to the Mountain Rescue Station for help. Tom Thomas radioed the Fire Station for back-up, before following Norman back to the hole.

Before long, Fireman Sam and Penny arrived on the scene. They had travelled in Penny's car, Venus, as the roads were very muddy.

"Let's get Mandy out quickly," said Sam. "There's a storm coming."

Penny and Tom quickly set up a winch over the hole, while Sam put on his safety harness.

"Right, I'm going in!" said Sam. "Lower me down, nice and slowly."

"Easy does it!" said Fireman Sam, as he was lowered down into the hole. Mandy was very pleased to see him!

"Don't worry, Mandy," smiled Sam. "We'll soon have you out!"

He lifted the harness and fastened it safely around Mandy, then called, "OK, Tom, pull her up!"

Tom used all his strength to slowly wind the winch,
until Mandy was safely back on the ground again.

"Phew! You're heavier than you look, Mandy!" he puffed.

Penny wrapped a blanket around Mandy, to keep her warm.

"OK, Sam," shouted Tom. "Your turn now!"

Everyone was warming up in Tom's Mountain Rescue cabin.

"You had a lucky escape," Sam said to Mandy. "But this wouldn't have happened if Norman hadn't borrowed my beep-o-matic."

"But what I can't understand is why Mandy was so heavy?" said Tom.

"Maybe it was because of these?" said Mandy. She turned out her pockets and lots of gold coins fell on to the floor!

"Half of the treasure is mine!" shouted Norman.

Great Fires of London! said Fireman Sam. "This is ancient gold. We'll have to take it to the Pontypandy Museum."

"Oh, no," groaned Norman. "That's the last time I go treasure-hunting with you, Mandy Flood!"

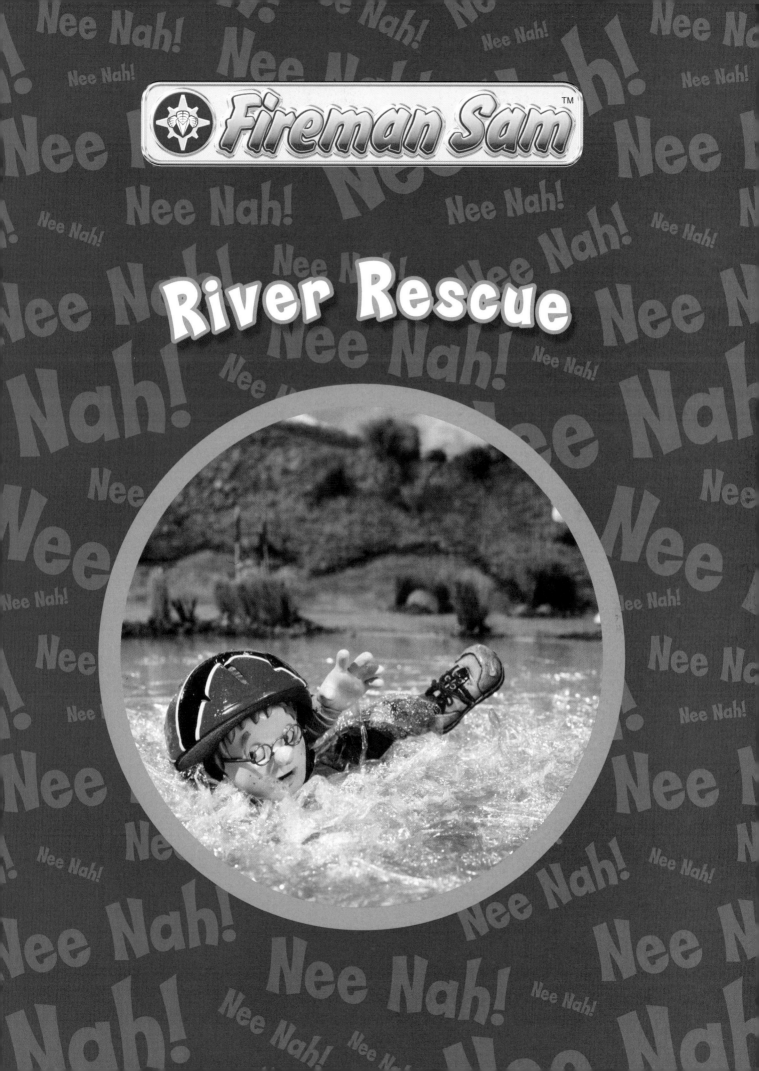

River Rescue

One day, Fireman Sam was fixing a puncture in one of Jupiter's tyres when Elvis came along. "Need any help, Sam?" asked Elvis.

But Sam shook his head. "No thanks, Elvis," he smiled.

Just then, James and Sarah arrived, carrying a deflated beach ball. "Rosa stuck her claws in our beach ball," said James. "Can you fix it?"

"I'll do it!" said Elvis, eagerly.

In the countryside, Tom Thomas was expertly flying a kite. Norman and Mandy were watching.

"Cor, that's a cool kite, Tom. Can I borrow it?" asked Norman.

"Sure, as long as you're careful with it," replied Tom.

"Careful's my middle name!" said Norman.

Tom wound in the kite and handed it to Norman.

At the Fire Station, Elvis had repaired the puncture for the twins.

"Now, men," said Officer Steele. "The sunshine will have people out on the water. Check all our safety equipment, including the pontoon."

"It's a sort of airbed for rescues on water," Sam explained to the twins.

But when Officer Steele went to get it from Jupiter's locker, the pontoon wasn't there!

Outside Dilys' shop, Norman was wearing his skateboarding helmet and knee pads, with a full bag of newspapers over his shoulder.

"Are you sure about this?" asked Mandy.

"With this little baby, I'll be able to do my newspaper round twice as fast!" replied Norman, tossing the kite into the air before speeding off.

"Hey, wait for me!" shouted Mandy, running after him.

Around the corner, Sarah and James were bouncing their ball.

"Have you seen Norman?" asked Mandy. The twins shook their heads.

"If you do, get out of the way!" laughed Mandy and off she went.

But just then, they heard Norman approaching –"**Wheee!**"

"Look out, James!" shouted Sarah.

Norman narrowly missed James. He sped straight past on his skateboard, before skidding out of control towards the lake.

"Aaargh!" cried Norman.

A big gust of wind caught the kite and lifted him over the lake. The wind dropped and Norman plunged into the water with a loud splash!

"Oh no!" cried Sarah and James. "Norman can't swim!"

At the Fire Station, Elvis had finally found the pontoon.

Meanwhile, Norman was struggling in the water. "Ah!" he shouted.

"I'll get Uncle Sam," said Sarah, and off she ran for help.

"Grab hold of this, Norman," said James and he threw him the beach ball. But it landed just out of Norman's reach!

Sarah's emergency message quickly reached the Fire Station.

"Oh no! Norman has been blown into the lake," said Sam.

"Scramble, men. Action Stations!" said Station Officer Steele.

Sam and Elvis put the inflatable pontoon in Jupiter's locker and the Fire Crew were ready. Nee Nah! Nee Nah! Penny followed in Venus.

Jupiter and Venus arrived at the lake with the Fire Crew.

"Inflate the pontoon, men!" said Station Officer Steele.

Sam and Elvis carefully unloaded the pontoon then Penny plugged it into Jupiter's generator. "Pontoon inflated, Sir," said Penny.

"We'll soon have you out of there, Norman!" said Sam.

Fireman Sam took his first swaying step on the inflatable pontoon towards Norman. The wind suddenly picked up, swaying the pontoon, and Sam was nearly knocked off balance!

"Wo-ow. Steady there. You alright?" asked Penny, anxiously.

"Yes, I'm fine, Penny," said Fireman Sam, giving her the thumbs-up.

"Hurry up, Sam. I think a fish has just swum up my trouser leg!" said Norman, as he clung to the rock.

"Hold on tight, Norman," said Sam. He lifted Norman onto the pontoon and carefully carried him to safety, as the pontoon swayed.

As Sam put Norman down onto the bank, a fish wriggled out of his jeans and back into the lake!

Dilys and Mandy were waiting by the shop when everyone got back.

"Next time you fly a kite, Norman, make sure to take care," said Sam.

"OK, Sam," said Norman. "And I'm definitely going to learn to swim."

"You've got to learn to float first," said Dilys, handing him arm bands.
"You can try these out in a nice hot bath."

"Oh, Mam!" cried Norman. And everyone laughed!

Goodbye!

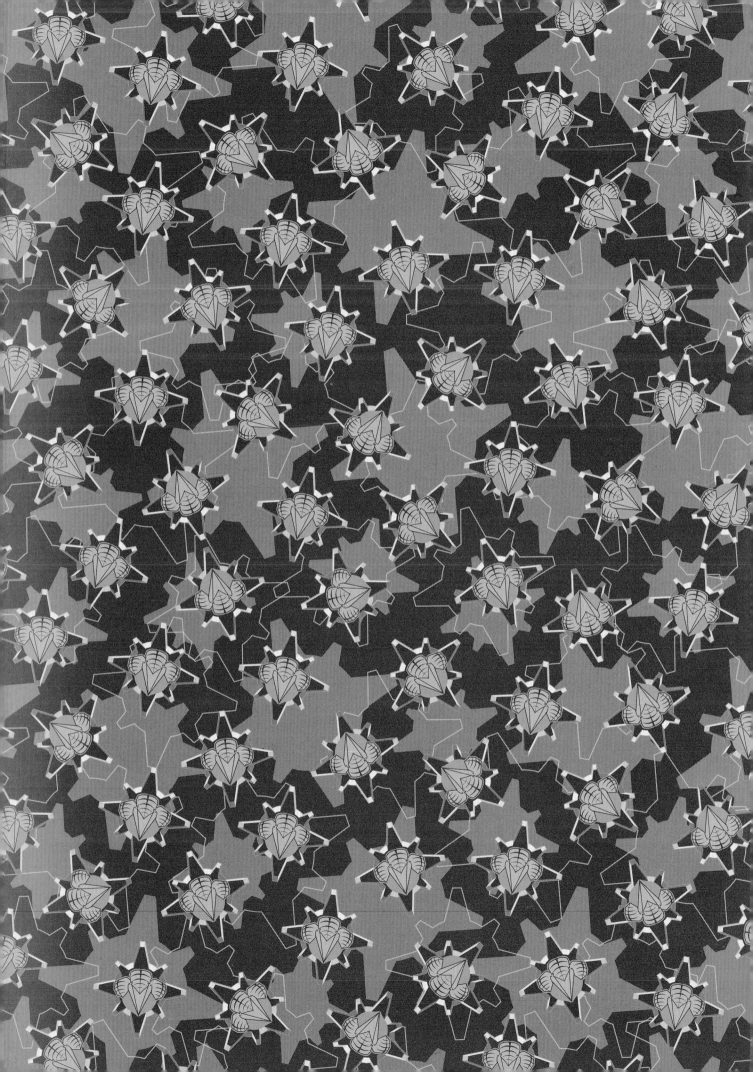